DATE ⌐

THE GHOST
OF J. STOKELY

by Bob Temple
illustrated by Shane Nitzsche

Librarian Reviewer
Marci Peschke
Librarian, Dallas Independent School District
MA Education Reading Specialist, Stephen F. Austin State University
Learning Resources Endorsement, Texas Women's University

Reading Consultant
Elizabeth Stedem
Educator/Consultant, Colorado Springs, CO
MA in Elementary Education, University of Denver, CO

STONE ARCH BOOKS
www.stonearchbooks.com

Shade Books are published by Stone Arch Books
151 Good Counsel Drive, P.O. Box 669
Mankato, Minnesota 56002
www.capstonepub.com

Library of Congress Cataloging-in-Publication Data
Temple, Bob.
    The Ghost of J. Stokely / by Bob Temple; illustrated by Shane
Nitzsche.
    p. cm. — (Shade Books)
    Summary: Seventeen-year-old Jared leads a group of younger
boys to Eagle Point, but their planned fishing trip turns into an
investigation of strange events surrounding the caretaker's cabin.
    ISBN 978-1-4342-0796-8 (library binding)
    ISBN 978-1-4342-0892-7 (pbk.)
    [1. Camps—Fiction. 2. Leadership—Fiction. 3. Mystery and
detective stories.] I. Nitzsche, Shane, ill. II. Title.
PZ7.T243Gho 2009
[Fic]—dc22   2008008005

Art Director: Heather Kindseth
Graphic Designer: Kay Fraser

Printed in the United States of America in Stevens Point, Wisconsin.
122009
005645R

...TABLE OF CONTENTS...

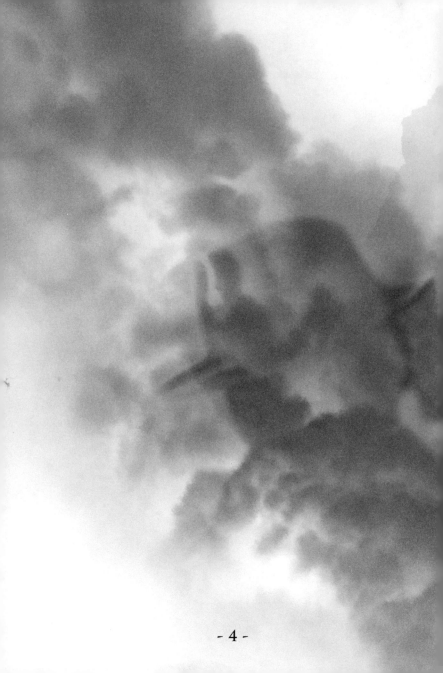

- CHAPTER 1 -
NO FOOTPRINTS

The dark figure of a man moved on the lonely beach. The only sound was a splash far out on the lake as an eagle soared down and scooped up a helpless fish.

The dark figure seemed not to hear. He moved slowly from one end of the beach to the other. Then he stopped, turned around, and walked across the beach again.

The beach was shaped like a triangle. Its sharpest end pointed toward the middle of Eagle Lake, so early explorers had named it Eagle Point.

Eagle Point was too far away from roads and highways to ever be a good location for a home. It was a great place for getting away from noise and crowds and cell phones. It was the perfect spot to set up a campsite and fish for pike, perch, and bluegills.

The figure on the beach did not seem interested in fishing or camping. He only seemed interested in moving and not staying still.

Someone watching this scene would have found it very strange. Not because the man never stopped walking, but because his feet left no footprints in the soft sand. As he stepped on pebbles and fallen twigs, he never made a single sound.

It was almost as if he wasn't there at all.

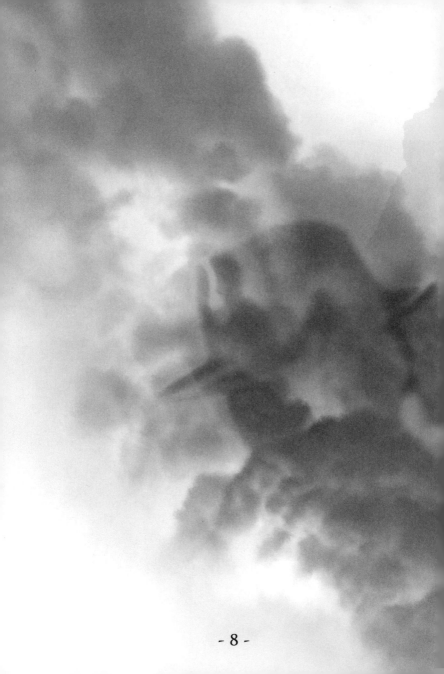

- CHAPTER 2 -
END OF THE ROAD

As he drove along the dusty forest road, Jared Holmes squinted and turned on his pickup's windshield wipers. The dust from his father's Jeep ahead of him was blurring the road.

The road twisted back and forth like a snake that couldn't make up its mind where it was going. Finally, his dad's brake lights shined red. Jared pulled up next to the Jeep.

He rolled down his side window. The road stopped in the middle of the woods.

"You've got to be kidding," said Jared. "This is it?" he asked his father.

Mr. Holmes smiled as he stepped out of the Jeep. "You've been to Waterville before," he said.

"It seemed a lot bigger," said Jared.

"That's because you were a lot smaller," said Mr. Holmes.

Jared looked around. All he saw were a few wooden buildings, a tiny gas station with a single gas pump, and a grocery store with a huge stuffed fish over the door. Only fifty feet away, sparkling through the trees, lay the southern end of Eagle Lake.

"Come on, guys, we don't have a lot of time," Mr. Holmes said as three boys climbed out of his Jeep. "Let's get these canoes down and get you on your way."

"That's right, guys," Jared said. "Gather up all the gear."

Jared's younger brother, Caleb, rolled his eyes. "Sure thing, boss," Caleb said.

"Is he going to be bossy the whole trip?" asked Luis, the taller one of Caleb's friends.

"Probably," said Caleb. "But he does know a lot about fishing."

Jared and Caleb spent a lot of time outdoors. Almost every weekend, they went fishing, hunting, camping, or canoeing with their father. This summer, Mr. Holmes had a work project that would keep him busy for the next few months. So Jared decided he would take his brother and his friends by himself. Jared had decided on a spot that he hadn't visited since he'd been in grade school — Eagle Point.

The only way to reach Eagle Point was by canoe. The old caretaker, Mr. Stokely, lived in a large cabin set back from the water. Jared's favorite camping spot was on the Point's hill, just above the pebbly beach. He had good memories of fishing there. The lake was filled with northern pike and huge walleye. Jared couldn't wait to get there.

Soon, the canoes were unloaded. Mr. Holmes leaned a hand against the Jeep. "You should have great fishing out by the Point this time of year," he said. Then he glanced at his watch. "Time for me to head back home. Do you have everything you need?"

Jared nodded. "We'll go to the outfitter's store for the last few supplies," he said. "I want to be on the water by noon, so we can reach Eagle Point by sundown."

"Good plan," said his father.

Jared had spent weeks preparing for the trip. He had it all planned out.

"Well, take care of your little brother," Mr. Holmes said. "I'll see you in a week."

As his father drove away, Jared turned to the younger guys. "Let's head to the store and get our last supplies," he said. "I think we still need a couple of things for the first-aid kit, too."

The four boys walked into the outfitter's store. It was a small, wood building with only two rooms, the store area and a small office. The store was lined with shelves filled with everything a camper or fisherman might need. Jared quickly found a can opener, a box of bandages, and some soap. Then he brought the items to the counter.

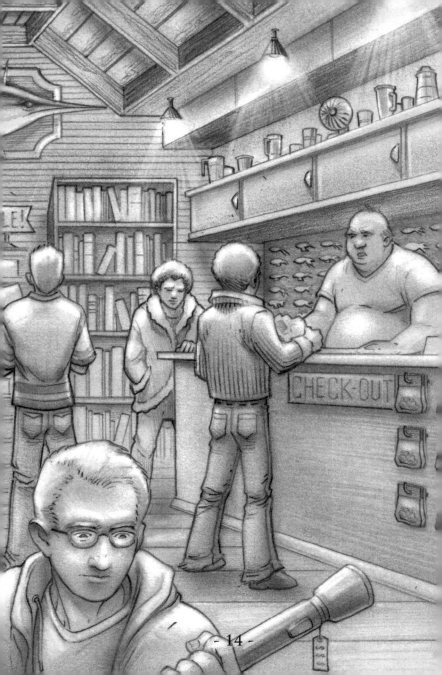

"What do we need soap for?" asked Caleb's friend Harry. "I thought this was a vacation."

Caleb rolled his eyes.

"Where are you boys headed?" the store clerk asked, smiling.

Jared piled his stuff onto the counter. "We're going up to Eagle Point," he said.

"Yeah, we'll be up there for a week," added Caleb.

The clerk suddenly turned pale. His smile disappeared. He looked at Jared and frowned.

"I don't think that's a good idea," the clerk said. "Unless you plan to fish for ghosts."

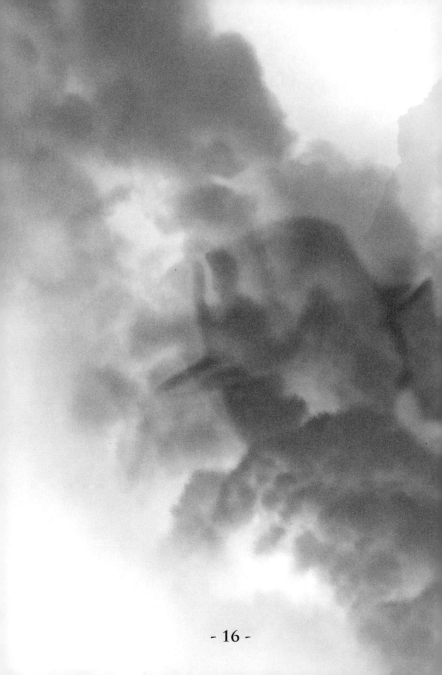

- CHAPTER 3 -
THE FOURTH MAN

"Ghosts?" repeated Caleb.

The store clerk nodded.

"You're kidding, right?" said Jared. "There's no such thing as ghosts."

The clerk said, "That's what I thought, kid. Before I went out there myself. But then . . . hang on." He turned and walked toward the office. "I'll be back."

Jared turned to the boys. "What was that all about?" he asked quietly.

"Maybe he's crazy," said Luis.

"Maybe we should camp somewhere else," Harry suggested.

They could hear the clerk banging through drawers and cupboards in the small office. He was hunting for something.

Luis laughed. "Harry, you never wanted to go on this trip," he said. "You're just trying to get out of it."

"Shhh," Jared said. "Listen."

The clerk was talking to someone in the next room. Jared couldn't hear the man, but he could tell he was upset.

Then the door swung open. "All right then," the store clerk said. His smile was back, but Jared thought it looked fake. "Here, I have something to show you."

The clerk opened up a big map of the area. It showed a huge series of lakes and streams.

"Here's where we are," the clerk said, pointing to a spot on the map. "Up here, to the north, is Eagle Point. Have you ever been there before?"

"Yes," Jared said.

"Tons of times," Caleb said.

The clerk moved his finger on the map to a place way over toward the east. "I think you should head over here," he said. "To a place called Skunk Hollow."

"Skunk Hollow?" Jared exclaimed. "Are you kidding me? The fishing is terrible there."

The clerk's smile disappeared again.

"Could you please tell me how much I owe you for this stuff?" Jared asked. "We've got to get going if we want to reach Eagle Point by sundown."

The clerk pulled out a photograph that had been hidden underneath the map. "I didn't want to have to show you this," he said. "But I think I better."

The boys crowded around to gaze down at the old photo in the clerk's hand. It showed three men standing on a beach. They were smiling. One of them was holding up a big fish. Behind them stood another man in a dark coat.

The fourth man must not have stood still for the photo. His face and body were blurry.

"What's this?" asked Jared.

"My buddies and I went fishing out at Eagle Point last year," said the clerk. He rang up the supplies and handed Jared the receipt. "We took that picture with a camera that had a timer. That way we could all be in the picture together."

"So?" said Caleb.

Jared nudged his brother. "Don't be rude," he whispered. Then he said in a louder voice to the clerk, "Yeah, so?"

"There were only three of us fishing on the Point that weekend," said the clerk. "Three."

Henry pointed a timid finger at the picture. "Then who's this guy in the back?"

"You tell me," said the clerk. "No one else was there."

Jared picked up their bag of supplies. "Good story," he said.

As the boys headed out the door, the clerk said angrily, "I told you, you're making a mistake. If you know what's good for you, don't go to Eagle Point."

Jared looked back at the clerk and frowned. Was the man threatening him? The two stared at each other.

"Listen," the man finally said. "Some strange things have been happening out there. Very strange things. I'd hate to see any of you kids get hurt."

Kids? Jared had heard enough. The man was trying to scare him, trying to make a fool of him in front of the younger guys. Jared gritted his teeth and headed out of the store. The door slammed behind him.

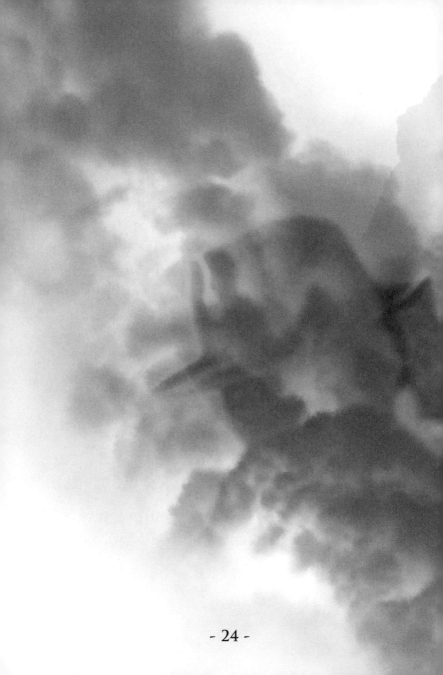

- CHAPTER 4 -
THE MISSING CABIN

Jared found the younger guys standing near the shore. "Come on, guys, let's load up the canoes," he said.

"We're still going?" Harry asked.

"Of course we're going," Caleb said. "We're not going to let that creep scare us."

Soon, they were getting into the canoes. Jared and Luis shared one canoe. Harry and Caleb shared the other. The boys paddled for more than an hour.

Harry complained the whole time. He said he was bored. He said he was tired. He said he wanted to turn around.

"I wouldn't even be here if my dad hadn't made me come," he kept saying.

"Maybe if you stop whining, you'll start to have fun," Caleb said.

"Just a couple more hours, guys," Jared said. "Soon we'll be making a turn. We'll go through some rapids there. After that, we'll be in Big Eagle Lake. Then we head to the north shore."

The afternoon sun was sliding down behind tall evergreens when Eagle Point finally came into view. A narrow piece of land lined with trees stuck out into the lake. In the dim light, the Point looked dark and lonely. They heard a splash.

"Maybe we shouldn't be up here," Harry said. "We need to turn back and go home."

"Stop it, Harry," Caleb said. "You're just trying to scare us."

"Listen, guys," Jared said. "It doesn't matter what that man said back at the store. He doesn't know what he's talking about. Eagle Point is a great place."

"Maybe it's different now," Harry said.

"Hey," said Luis, nodding toward the Point. "I thought you said there was a house out there."

"There is. It's Mr. Stokely's," said Jared. "He's the caretaker. He has a cabin nearby."

As they got closer to Eagle Point, Jared realized that something was different. "Where are the docks?" he said. "There used to be two old wooden docks right here."

As he paddled up to shore, Jared looked down and peered through the clear water. The boards from the dock were at the bottom of the lake, burned and broken.

Jared and Caleb quickly pulled the canoes onto the beach. Then Jared turned to Luis and Harry and said, "Stay here."

He and Caleb headed toward Mr. Stokely's cabin. As fast as they could, they climbed the steep hill. Jared, who was faster and stronger, reached the top of the hill first. Then he stopped in his tracks.

"What is it?" Caleb yelled. "What's the matter?"

But Jared couldn't speak. The caretaker's cabin — home to so many great memories, home to Mr. Stokely — was gone.

It had burned to the ground.

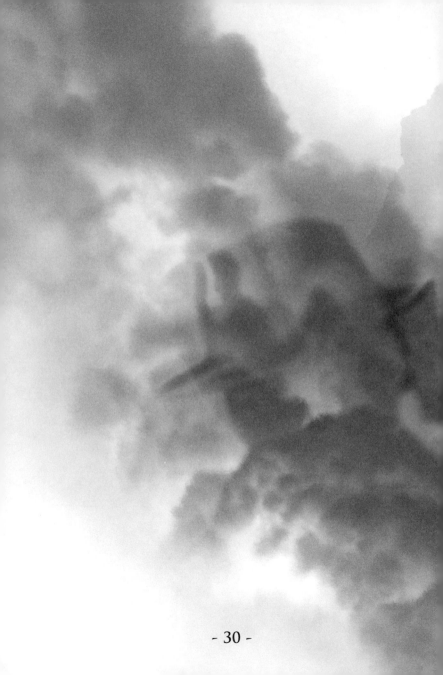

- CHAPTER 5 -
NOISES AT NIGHT

Jared didn't know what to do. Then Luis and Harry ran up the hill. Luis looked at the burnt remains of the cabin and gave a long, low whistle.

"Whoa! What happened here?" Harry said.

Luis laughed. "What do you think happened?" he said. "There was a fire."

"I thought you said this was a nice place," said Harry.

"It was," Jared said. His voice was filled with shock and sadness. "It really was."

"Okay, that's it," Harry said. "Let's get back in the canoes and get out of here as fast as we can."

"We need to find out what happened here," said Jared.

"And what happened to Mr. Stokely," Caleb added.

The boys were quiet for a few minutes. Two walls of the cabin were still standing, although they were black from the smoke and flames. A few small plants were growing around the area. The fire must have happened months before.

"Do you think there's a body in there?" asked Harry.

"Be quiet, Harry," said Jared.

Finally, Luis asked, "Well, what's the plan?"

"Yeah, boss," said Caleb, looking up at his brother. "What's the plan?"

"We'll pitch the tents," Jared said. "But not up here. I think we should camp lower down, just off the beach. Let's eat dinner and chill out for the night. In the morning, we can look around."

They set up two tents. Luis and Harry would share one, and Caleb and Jared would share the other. The long day of paddling had tired them out, so after dinner they fell asleep quickly.

As he drifted off to sleep, Jared wondered about the store clerk. Why hadn't he told them about the fire at the cabin?

Maybe the clerk didn't know. Maybe Mr. Stokely's place had been fine when the clerk and his buddies fished here last year.

In the middle of the night, a noise woke Jared. It was a rustling in the bushes. He could hear the sound of twigs snapping. Then he heard a thud, and then a strange, hoarse call. What was going on?

Jared grabbed his flashlight. He unzipped his tent and stepped out into the moonlight. Caleb was already outside, standing between the tents.

"Did you hear that?" Caleb asked. His voice was barely louder than a whisper.

"What is it?" Jared whispered back.

Then the noise came again. It sounded like it was coming from the path that led to the lakeshore.

Caleb and Jared looked at each other. They slowly stepped toward the path.

In the moonlight, they saw a figure fifty feet ahead of them. A man was walking toward the lakeshore, toward their canoes.

"Let's follow him," said Jared.

The path wound around a few trees and bushes, and then led out onto the pebbly beach. The brothers hurried after the figure. When they reached the beach, Jared let out a sigh of relief. Their canoes were still there, pulled up onto the rocks and grass.

"Where is he?" asked Caleb.

Jared looked from side to side. Moonlight lit up the entire shore of the lake. The beach was wide and long. It was also empty. The man was nowhere to be seen.

Where did he go? Jared wondered.

Then they heard a scream coming from the campsite.

It was Harry.

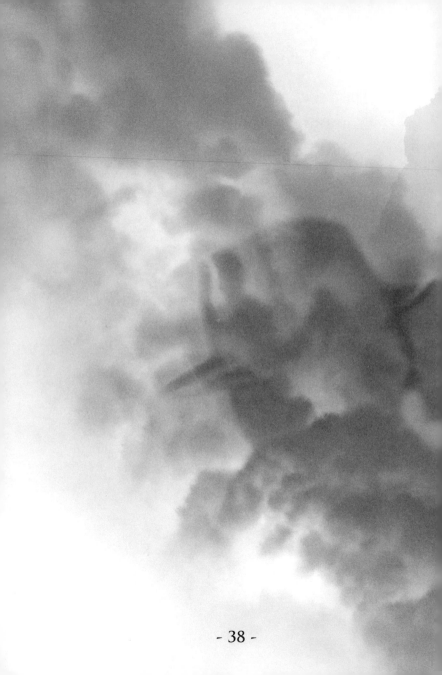

- CHAPTER 6 -
CRASH!

Jared and Caleb ran back to their tents. "Harry!" yelled Caleb. "Where are you?"

Luis popped his head out of his tent. "What's going on?" he said, sleepily. "Why are you guys yelling?"

Harry ran into the campsite, gasping. "There's a man!" he yelled. "I saw a man out there!"

"Where?" asked Jared. "Try to calm down. Take a deep breath."

Harry bent over, trying to catch his breath. He pointed toward a dark group of trees.

Jared ran toward the trees. Caleb stood where he was and folded his arms.

"What were you doing?" Caleb asked suspiciously.

"I was in the woods," Harry said. "You know . . . going to the bathroom. And while I was standing there, all of a sudden I looked up. And there was a guy right there. Staring at me."

"Who was he?" asked Luis.

"How should I know?" said Harry. "He was some old guy wearing glasses."

"You got freaked out by some old fisherman?" said Luis.

Jared sprinted back to the campsite. "I don't see anyone out there," he said.

"Harry's seeing things," said Luis.

"He said some old guy wearing glasses was watching him," added Caleb.

Jared was quiet. He remembered that old Mr. Stokely had worn glasses.

"I'm not making it up!" shouted Harry. "I saw him."

Then, from behind them, they heard another noise. First came a creaking sound, then a series of loud pops.

Jared knew that noise. "Timber!" he yelled.

Jared grabbed Caleb's arm and dove for the brush, pulling his younger brother behind him. Luis and Harry followed.

Crash!

The trunk of a tall, dead tree fell behind them. It fell between the two tents. It fell right where the boys had been standing.

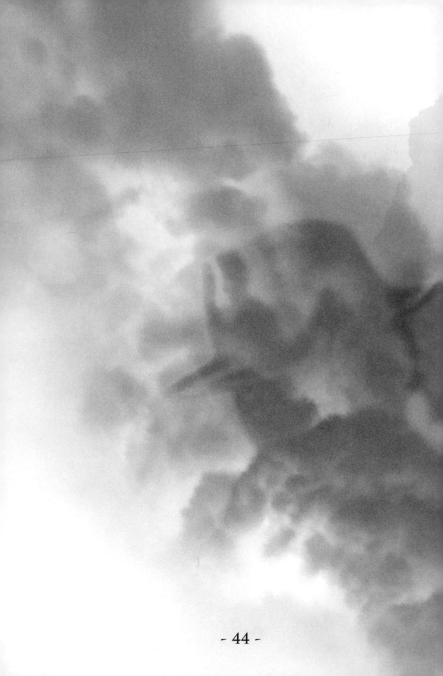

- CHAPTER 7 -
THE WARNING

No one slept for the rest of the night. They dragged their sleeping bags onto the beach. They wanted to sleep far away from any trees.

Every noise seemed scary and kept them awake. Every rustle of the wind through the pine needles made them jump.

Jared had tried to calm them down. "Everything's okay. The fire that burned the cabin probably weakened the tree. That's why it fell down," he'd said.

"What about the ghost?" Harry had asked.

Jared told them there was no ghost. That was crazy. There was no such thing as ghosts. Harry had probably just seen a shadow. It was a trick of the moonlight.

But as Jared lay in his sleeping bag and stared at the stars overhead, he was worried. Had Harry seen the ghost of Mr. Stokely? Was it the same ghost that appeared as the blurry, dark figure in the store clerk's photo? If it was Mr. Stokely's ghost, what had happened to Mr. Stokely?

At dawn, none of the boys wanted to go fishing. Instead, Jared told them to head out in different directions and look for clues. Broken branches, trash, anything that could mean someone had been there.

Jared decided that he would go check out the cabin fire. He told everyone to report back in two hours — earlier if they found something really interesting.

The boys searched for two hours, but found nothing. They were tired and hungry. Jared decided that everyone would feel better if they ate something. All the food was in his tent, so he crawled inside to get it. As he crawled in, the other boys heard him gasp.

"What? What is it?" Caleb yelled. He quickly crawled inside the tent. Jared didn't move. He was holding a piece of paper. He was too scared to speak.

Caleb snatched the paper from Jared's hands. "Go back. This land is cursed," he read in a shaky voice.

Caleb crawled quickly out of the tent and pointed at Harry. "You're doing this!" he cried.

"You're crazy!" Harry shouted.

"You could have left the note when the rest of us were out hunting for clues," Caleb said. "Admit it. You never wanted to come here in the first place."

"You're right," Harry said. "I didn't want to come here. But I didn't do any of this stuff. Besides, how would I make that tree fall, huh?" He clenched his fists and moved closer to Caleb.

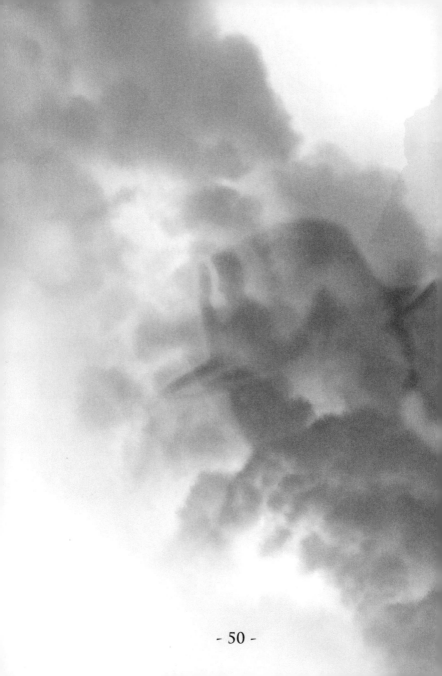

- CHAPTER 8 -
CAMP FIRE

"Stop it!" Jared yelled. "We need to work together to figure this out." Then he added, more quietly, "So, come on. Everyone just needs to settle down."

Jared wasn't able to convince Luis or Caleb that Harry was innocent. All he could do was keep Harry by his side for the rest of the day. He was worried that the boys would get into a fight otherwise.

All day long, the four looked all over Eagle Point for clues. No one found a thing.

They did learn that the tree that had fallen into their campsite was not burned. The tree hadn't been chopped with an ax, either.

It was simply an old dead tree. It was ready to fall. All of the other trees near the campsite were fine.

Finally, they decided to call it a night. Caleb and Jared built a campfire, and they all settled in around it.

"There's something weird about the cabin burning down," Jared said. "It wasn't a wildfire, since only the cabin and the docks were burned. How does a dock catch on fire when it's sitting in the water?"

"Maybe the old caretaker burned it down," Luis said.

"What do you mean?" Jared asked.

"Maybe he got sick of running the place," Luis explained. "Maybe he burned it down and took off."

"No way," Caleb said. "Mr. Stokely loved it here. He never would have done something like that."

"Or maybe Stokely got caught in the fire," said Harry. "And that's why his ghost is still haunting this place."

"Knock it off," said Luis.

"That's a pretty crazy idea," Caleb said.

Jared stared at the campfire. Maybe Harry was right. Maybe Mr. Stokely had been killed in the cabin fire. That thought made him really sad.

They ate a quick dinner of hot dogs and beans. Then the boys returned to their tents.

They decided that a second tree was not going to fall into the camp. Even Harry admitted that would be too weird.

That night, Caleb moved in with Luis. They both still thought that Harry had somehow made the tree fall. Harry moved his stuff into Jared's tent. They didn't talk before they fell asleep.

Later that night, Jared woke up when he heard a whisper from outside his tent. "Come out," the voice said. "Come out."

Jared turned on his flashlight and shone it at Harry's sleeping bag. It was empty.

"Quit it, Harry," Jared said. "I know that's you."

"Come out," the voice whispered again.

Fear shot through Jared. That voice was not Harry's.

With shaking fingers, Jared unzipped his tent and crawled out. Carefully, he got to his feet.

As he stood up, he saw the shadowy figure of a man in the moonlight, a few yards away. The man was too tall to be Harry.

The man held out his hand. Then he said, "Leave in the morning. Forget what you saw here and no harm will come to you. Stay another day, and this promise is no good."

Jared saw a flash of light out of the corner of his eye. When he turned, he saw his tent going up in flames.

Jared yelled out and rushed to the tent. Caleb and Luis scrambled out of their own tent when they heard the screams.

They tried to put out the flames, but it was too late. Jared's tent was completely burned.

"It's a good thing you weren't inside when it started," said Caleb.

"I don't believe this," said Jared. Then he turned toward the shadows. The man was gone.

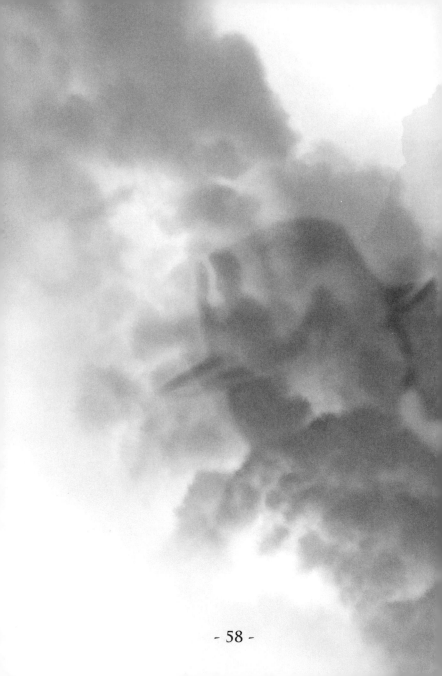

- CHAPTER 9 -
THE SHADOW

Jared suddenly got angry. Ghost or no ghost, he ran toward the spot where the man had last been standing and crashed through the woods. He pushed aside bushes and tree branches, ignoring the sharp twigs that scratched his skin.

There! A dark figure was running ahead of him. Jared leaped toward the shadow.

Jared's arms got tangled up with a pair of legs. The shadow fell into a thick bush.

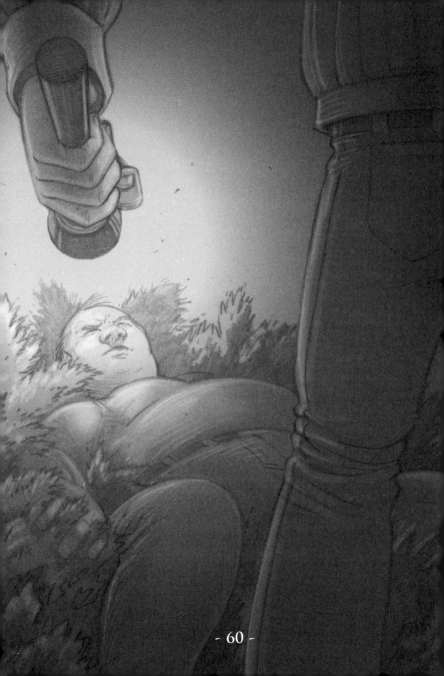

Quickly, Jared got to his feet. "You're no ghost!" he shouted.

The man staring up at Jared was the clerk from the outfitter's store back in Waterville.

"You shouldn't be here," said the clerk.

"What's going on here?" came another voice. It was Caleb. He had followed his older brother through the woods. "Hey, it's that crazy guy from the store," he said.

"Get out of here," yelled the clerk.

"Not until you tell us what's going on here," Jared demanded.

"He's the ghost!" said Caleb.

The clerk said nothing.

"Why are you doing this?" asked Jared. "Because of what happened to Mr. Stokely?"

"Is it because of the fire?" asked Caleb.

The clerk turned his head away from them. "It was an accident," he said. "It was a stupid prank that got out of control."

"You set the fire?" asked Jared.

The clerk ignored them and went on. "Stokely was always telling us what we could and couldn't do. He wrecked all of our fun. So what if we caught a few more fish than was allowed? What's the big deal? But Stokely said he'd tell the police, and then me and my buddies would get into serious trouble."

The clerk pulled himself into a sitting position on the ground. "Stokely was in his cabin," he said. "We just thought we'd scare him. It wasn't my idea, but I guess I went along with it."

"What happened?" asked Jared.

"We told him we were going to burn down his cabin. We were only going to scare him a little. He was always getting in our way, so we thought we'd teach him a lesson. Maybe he'd leave us alone in the future," the clerk explained.

He paused. Then he said, "Stokely went inside his house. But then one of the guys dropped a torch he was carrying. It fell on Stokely's porch. That wood was so old and dry, it started to spread real fast. We just ran and got out of there."

"What happened to Mr. Stokely?" Caleb asked quietly.

The clerk shook his head. "I don't know. The old fool must have locked himself in his cabin. It didn't have a back door, either."

"He was trapped," said Jared.

"It was an accident," the clerk repeated.

A scream came from the campsite.

"Not again," said Caleb. "Harry is afraid of his own shadow."

"We better check it out," said Jared.

The two brothers headed back through the woods. As they pushed through the last few trees, they saw their friends standing there. The two boys were stiff and frozen with fear.

"What's wrong?" asked Caleb.

Luis and Harry pointed past their tent. A man was standing there. He was at least ten feet tall. His face was hidden in the shadows of the trees. Moonlight gleamed on his glasses.

The hair on the back of Jared's neck stood up. Goosebumps shot down his spine. "Mr. Stokely?" he whispered.

The huge shadow raised its right arm. Dark fingers pointed toward them.

"You!" came a strange voice.

"Me?" squeaked Harry.

"You!" someone yelled.

The boys all turned around. The clerk from the outfitter's store had followed Jared and Caleb. He had been silently standing behind them the whole time. Even in the dim light of the boys' dying campfire, they could see that his face was pale with fear.

"Stokely," the clerk croaked.

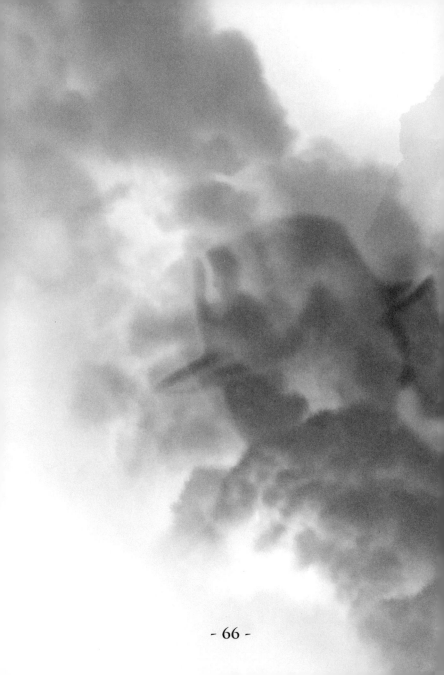

CHAPTER 10

REVENGE

The dark shadow seemed to grow even taller. It towered at least twenty feet above them. Its head was lost in the shadows of overhead pine branches.

Behind the figure, a strange light glowed. Red flames danced on the bushes. The reddish light lit up the campsite, but it made the shadowy man appear even darker than before.

"Fire!" yelled Caleb.

The flames raced up the trunks of the trees surrounding the campsite. Ashes and burning chunks of wood rained down on the boys. As fast as they could, they ran along the path that led to the shore.

Behind them, the fire spread quickly. Trees were blazing like candles. Jared could feel the heat of the fire on the back of his neck as he ran along the path.

"Head to the canoes!" he yelled.

When they reached the shoreline, the boys froze. Their canoes were gone!

"That creepy clerk did this," said Caleb. "Now we'll die just like old Stokely did!"

"Look!" shouted Harry. He pointed farther down the shore. "There's a canoe over there. It's not ours, but who cares!"

The boys ran to the canoe and jumped inside. "Quick, push off," ordered Jared.

Within seconds, the boys had paddled the canoe thirty feet from shore. The fire spread across Eagle Point. The crackling of flames and the crashing of burnt timber echoed across the lake.

"Wow! That is incredible," said Harry.

"Where's that store guy?" said Caleb.

Another tree crashed onto the point, its branches blazing.

"He's trapped," said Jared. "Trapped like Mr. Stokely was trapped."

"Maybe he escaped," said Harry. "Maybe he had a boat hidden somewhere."

"Maybe," said Jared. But he doubted it.

"Speaking of the canoe, look at this," said Luis. He held up an old life preserver. "It was under my seat," he added.

The life preserver was stamped with words:

EAGLE POINT CAMPGROUND

J. Stokely, Caretaker

"That ghost saved our lives," said Caleb.

"There's no such thing as ghosts," Jared said.

"But Jared—" exclaimed his brother.

"Just keep paddling," said Jared, quietly. None of the boys spoke for the rest of the journey. The starlight provided enough light for them to travel by. When dawn broke, they could see the outlines of the outfitter's store in Waterville.

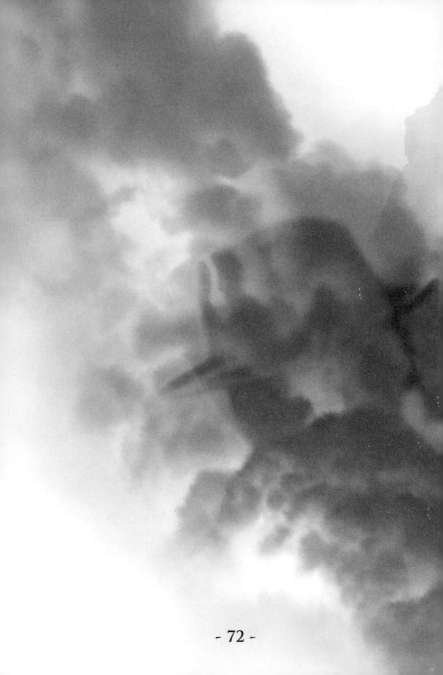

THE POINT

The next morning, gray clouds hung above Eagle Point.

It was a calm morning. Tall evergreens pointed toward the sky. Gentle waves lapped against the pebbly shore.

A breeze blew through the bushes. It rustled the dark green leaves.

There were no signs that a wildfire had ever burned on that part of the shore.

The dark figures of two men moved on the lonely beach. The only sound was the splash far out on the lake as an eagle soared down and scooped up a helpless fish.

The dark figures seemed not to hear. They moved slowly and carefully from one end of the beach to the other.

As they stepped on pebbles and fallen twigs, the two shadows never made a single sound. They didn't leave footprints. It was almost as if they weren't even there.

About the Author

Bob Temple lives in Rosemount, Minnesota, with his wife and three children. He has written more than thirty books for children. Over the years, he has coached more than twenty kids' soccer, basketball, and baseball teams. He also loves visiting classrooms to talk about his writing.

About the Illustrator

Shane Nitzsche has been creating artwork since he could wrap his little fingers around a pencil, but he really started to take it seriously after he cracked open his first comic book. Shane spent his younger years in rural Missouri, but has since moved to Portland, Oregon and can't think of any better place in the world to continue pursuing his career. (Oh, and that last name? It's pronounced NIT-chee.)

Glossary

canoe (kuh-NOO)—a narrow boat that you can move through the water by paddling

caretaker (KAIR-tay-kur)—someone whose job it is to look after something

clerk (KLURK)—a salesperson in a store

cursed (KURSD)—if something or someone is cursed, it will experience bad luck

dock (DOK)—a place where boats or canoes load and unload

figure (FIG-yur)—a person's shape

innocent (IN-uh-suhnt)—not guilty

lakeshore (LAKE-shor)—the edge of a lake

life preserver (LIFE pri-ZURV-er)—a ring that can be filled with air and used to keep a person afloat in water.

outfitter's store (OUT-fit-turz STOR)—a store where things are sold for camping, hunting, or fishing

prank (PRANGK)—a trick

Discussion Questions

1. Did the boys do anything wrong or break any rules in this book? Talk about your answer.

2. Do you believe in ghosts? Why or why not?

3. Do you think that Jared and the other boys will ever return to Eagle Point? Explain your answer.

Writing Prompts

1. If you could go anywhere for a fun summer vacation with your friends, where would you go? What would you do there?

2. Sometimes it can be interesting to think about a story from another person's point of view. Try writing chapter 9 from the clerk's point of view. What does he see and hear? What does he think about?

3. This book is a ghost story. Write your own ghost story!

Internet Sites

Do you want to know more about subjects related to this book? Or are you interested in learning about other topics? Then check out FactHound, a fun, easy way to find Internet sites.

Our investigative staff has already sniffed out great sites for you!

Here's how to use FactHound:

1. Visit *www.facthound.com*

2. Select your grade level.

3. To learn more about subjects related to this book, type in the book's ISBN number: **9781434207968**.

4. Click the **Fetch It** button.

FactHound will fetch the best Internet sites for you!